DOCTOR · WHO

DECIDE YOUR DESTINY

BBC CHILDREN'S BOOKS
Published by the Penguin Group
Penguin Books Ltd, 80 Strand, London, WC2R 0RL, England
Penguin Group (USA) Inc., 375 Hudson Street, New York, New York 10014, USA
Penguin Books (Australia) Ltd, 250 Camberwell Road, Camberwell, Victoria 3124, Australia.
(A division of Pearson Australia Group Pty Ltd)
Canada, India, New Zealand, South Africa
Published by BBC Children's Books, 2007
Text and design © Children's Character Books, 2007
Written by Richard Dungworth
2
ISBN-13: 978-1-40590-352-3
ISBN-10: 1-40590-352-X
Printed in Great Britain by Clays Ltd, St Ives plc

DECIDE YOUR DESTINY

Alien Arena

by Richard Dungworth

Alien Arena

1 You are strolling to school one damp morning, when you are suddenly aware of a peculiar tingling sensation all over your skin. It rapidly intensifies, until your entire nervous system is fizzing with electrical energy. An instant later, you are blinded by a flare of intense white light.

As the pins-and-needles subside, your vision gradually returns. You are alarmed to find that your entire surroundings have transformed. You are now standing on a raised circular platform, encircled by tall, thin transparent columns. Each is filled with purple fluid, through which bubbles rise at regular intervals. The platform is at the centre of a circular, white-walled room, crammed with technical-looking equipment.

'You imbecile!'

Beside a nearby control console stands a remarkably short man — clearly an adult, but not more than four feet tall. He is angrily addressing his companion, who is unlike any being you have seen before. The creature is twice the man's height, remarkably thin, with six insect-like limbs. Its features are dominated by a pair of gigantic, startled-looking eyes. And its entire body is tangerine.

'I told you to select a legendary human warrior — not a puny child!'

The giant orange grasshopper-thing is clearly terrified.

'I sorry, Meester Beeg. Eet not verk dees time. I try again — ve get beeg Earth bossman who fight plenty plenty.'

'You better had, you fool,' snarls the small man (evidently called 'Mr Big'). 'Set up another Extraction as soon as possible.' He thrusts a finger at you. 'But first, get rid of that.'

'Yes Meester Beeg, I do eet very right away,' grovels the grasshopper as the angry dwarf storms from the room. The creature prises a prod-like implement with a pulsing blue end from a rack on the wall, and crosses the room towards you.

To make a dash for the doorway, go to 66.
To reason with the grasshopper creature, go to 52.

2 The material from which the sphere is made fascinates you. It's like some sort of gemstone, the blackest of blacks. But as you reach out to touch its ultra-smooth surface, a pinpoint of bright green light suddenly blossoms at the heart of the sphere. An instant later a prompt in luminous green letters is projected onto its curving surface:

SELECT TRANSIT DESTINATION:
1 PRISONER EXERCISE AREA
2 STAFF KITCHEN
3 WASTE PROCESSING

Intrigued, you tentatively touch the top option. A second message replaces the first:

DESTINATION SELECTED: TRANSIT BAY ACTIVE

With a gentle hiss, a section of the corridor wall behind you suddenly lifts, and slides sideways to reveal a previously invisible doorway.

To catch up with Martha, go to 51. To go through the revealed doorway, go to 29.

3 $\quad$ **B**y clinging to your monstrous opponent's back, you have managed to find the one place where it cannot strike at you with its lethal tail or claws. But it is hardly a comfortable refuge. Your enemy is livid at your cunning ploy, and thrashes about wildly in an attempt to shake you off. Somehow, you cling on.

Determined to dislodge you, the creature tries another tactic. It backs towards the nearest section of the Arena's perimeter, and rears up, in an attempt to crush you against the wall.

As you fight to endure your battering, you realize that from your elevated position on your enemy's back, you could probably reach the top of the Arena wall.

To continue to cling on for dear life, go to 89. To attempt to scramble over the Arena wall, go to 57.

4 While the Doctor investigates the several corridors radiating from the hub, you examine the mislaid gadget. It has a small video screen and keypad. The display shows the view along an empty corridor, under the heading 'Sector K44'.

As you try the keypad, the heading changes to 'Sector K45', and a new image appears. You can clearly see — and hear — three figures: two alien convicts, roughly shoving Martha through the doorway of a small cell. As you watch on the hand-held device, the aliens close and lock the cell door, then take up sentry positions on either side of it.

The Doctor returns from checking out the third corridor, looking excited.

'Jackpot! This one leads to some sort of confinement area — Sector K45, it says.'

To keep watch on the surveillance device for a chance to rescue Martha, go to 32. To head for the cells, along the third corridor, go to 87.

5 To your great relief, it's only the Doctor.

'I've found Sector K45 — Martha's in Cell 17, guarded by a couple of Big's convict cronies. Just popped back to the TARDIS for these.'

He holds up what appear to be several Christmas tree baubles, before throwing one down each of the waste chutes.

'I can detonate them remotely. Might come in handy if we need a diversion.'

Without further explanation, the Doctor leads you stealthily along several passageways, till you find yourself at a junction of two corridors lined with cells. As you peer around the corner, you see a door marked '17', guarded by two heavily-armed convicts.

'What do you reckon?' whispers the Doctor. 'We can lie low and wait it out. Or we can see if a few loud bangs get their attention…'

To watch and wait, go to 32. To try the Doctor's diversion plan, go to 94.

6 | You release your grip on the creature's thrashing forelimb, and are flung high into the air, travelling some distance across the Arena before coming back down to earth with a bruising bump. You hurry to regain your feet, aware that your multi-limbed foe is already closing in for another attack.

On the ground beside you, to your great delight, lies a long double-handed sword. Martha has clearly had some success in disarming her fierce opponent. You quickly grab its hilt, and use every ounce of your fading strength to lift it high, as your opponent bears down upon you once more.

To use the sword defensively, to fend off your opponent's claws, go to 72. To try one all-out, berserker-style attack, go to 8.

7 The Doctor rummages in an inside pocket and pulls out two pairs of cardboard 3-D spectacles.

'Wear these,' he says, handing you one pair, and putting on the other himself. 'Now then… lights off…'

He touches the control screen, and your surroundings are suddenly plunged into pitch blackness. The spectacles, however, enable you to see, albeit in a strange green/black monotone.

The Doctor quietly opens the exit hatch and you follow him down the ladder. The convicts below are blundering about helplessly in the total darkness. You slip silently past, undetected.

Following the corridor along which Martha was dragged, you come to a pair of sliding doors, which open automatically. Beyond them lies a new sector, with its lighting still activated. In the open doorway stand two tough-looking aliens.

To fight your way past, go to 26. To run for it, go to 44.

8 Your fierce attack only angers your opponent. But before it can retaliate, you are both distracted by a strange, oscillating sound. The TARDIS gradually materialises within the Arena, metres from where you stand. The Doctor steps casually out. A small globe of what looks like blue jelly hovers beside his shoulder. Jal-Neth, too, is with him.

The Doctor addresses the bewildered crowd.

'Fight's over, I'm afraid. Sorry to spoil the party. If you could surrender your weapons and make your way quietly back to your original cells, we'd be much obliged.'

Mr Big guffaws loudly. 'And if we don't, Doctor? Are you and your friends going to overpower us?'

Contemptuous laughter fills the Arena, but the Doctor remains unfazed.

'Your concept of 'power' is very naïve, Mr Big — as your choice of Tyrants of Time clearly shows. You don't have to be a muscle-bound thug to have clout. I've just picked up an old friend from the Perrazoic Era to illustrate my point.' The Doctor gestures to the floating jelly ball.

'May I introduce Balbaljo Za, member of the Tronynx Peace Council.'

'We're supposed to be frightened of that?' scoffs Mr Big.

'The Tronynx are potent telepaths,' explains the Doctor. 'They can control multiple minds at will. Councillor Za has no need of physical dominance to make you do exactly as she wishes.'

'Enough of this nonsense!' screams Mr Big. 'Kill them!'

At that moment, a luminous glow blooms at the heart of the small blue globe. To your amazement, each and every one of the convicts and warriors instantly falls silent and still, zombie-like.

The Doctor nods courteously to the blue globe. 'Thank you, Councillor.' Then he turns towards you. 'Now, my young friend, once we've helped Jal-Neth put things straight here, I'd better take you home.' He scans the dazed Tyrants of Time caged around the Arena, then grins at you. 'Though we will need to drop off a few friends on the way...'

This adventure in time and space is over.

9 Your efforts are in vain — you soon find yourself a captive of your convict enemies. They escort you to a luxurious lounge area, where Mr Big is slouched in a recliner.

'Given us quite a runaround, haven't you?' sneers Big. 'Such fighting spirit deserves recognition — which is why you'll be the opening act in the Arena tonight. Now — which of our 'Tyrants of Time' would you like a shot at?'

Big places a tiny green prism on his outstretched palm. A 3-D projection of a miniature Mongolian warrior immediately appears above it.

'Genghis Khan, perhaps? Or someone less... terrestrial?' He rotates the prism several times. At each rotation, a different, inhuman creature appears in miniature. You cringe at the sight of a monstrous, scorpion-like beast.

'Ah, our arachnid friend Scorantulus interests you? His poisonous tail-sting helped him sustain a rule of terror over the planet of Tharos for three hundred years. Most of our warriors compete because otherwise they receive no food. But for Scorantulus, the opposition is the food...'

Another group of convicts suddenly enter, dragging Martha with them.

'Ah!' leers Big. 'And for your friend here, a lady, I think.' He turns the prism again and an imposing blue-skinned woman appears. 'Why not your very own Boudicca, warrior-chieftain of the first century? Few females from any galaxy have surpassed her skill-at-arms.'

He turns to his guards. 'Equip them, and take them to the Arena.'

◆ ◆ ◆

Less than an hour later, you find yourself standing at the centre of a makeshift amphitheatre, surrounded by a crowd of jeering ex-convicts. Martha stands a short distance away. Like you, she has a small wooden shield in her grasp.

All around the Arena's walled perimeter stand sealed transparent cubes, each containing one of Big's 'Tyrants of Time'. Two stand open. Advancing towards Martha from the first is Boudicca, ancient warrior Queen. From the other, the giant scorpion-like monster from Tharos is rapidly scuttling your way.

To attack Scorantulus with your shield, go to 65. To concentrate on avoiding him, go to 11.

---

10 You scramble wildly across the floor towards where your sword lies. But as you try to recover the weapon, your insect-eyed opponent seizes the opportunity to attack. It lunges violently at you with the lethal laser tip of its fighting staff.

Thankfully, you are agile enough to dodge at the last minute. As the deadly tip narrowly misses your side, you quickly grab the shaft of your enemy's weapon and give it a sharp tug. Caught off balance, your enemy stumbles and falls forward.

The creature's crystalline armour clatters loudly as it hits the deck, emitting a maddened wail as its grotesque, segmented eye slams into the Arena floor.

To grab your sword and attack while your opponent is vulnerable, go to 8. To put some distance between you and the insect-eyed monster before it regains its feet, go to 46.

11 You hurry away from your deadly-tailed adversary – only to blunder headlong into the fight raging between Martha and her formidable opponent.

'Look out!' shrieks Martha, too late, as the angry warrior takes a vicious swing with their mighty fist, sending you reeling.

You lie on the Arena floor dazed, unable to do anything as your own opponent moves in for the kill. When your senses return, it is only in time to see your enemy preparing a final strike with its terrible tail, and to hear the crowd baying for blood.

Suddenly, a heavy wooden disc hits the creature hard in the face, temporarily stunning it. Martha has flung her shield at your enemy, in a last ditch attempt to save your skin.

'Now RUN!' she yells, dodging yet another strike from her own opponent.

To scramble onto the creature's back while it is stunned, go to 3. To take Martha's advice, go to 84.

12 You dash past the scorpion-creature's side, attempting to get behind it. But it wheels quickly round, its grotesque limbs rattling on the Arena floor. As you sprint towards the edge of the Arena, it comes scuttling after you, easily matching your pace.

The creature lifts its tail-end in preparation for another attack. In desperation, you dive for cover into the vacant transparent cube from which your monstrous opponent originally emerged, just as it strikes with its deadly sting.

The creature's tail crashes down on the roof of the cube, which shatters in an explosion of jagged shards. As the debris rains down, you hear the creature give an agonized hiss. One long, needle-sharp shard has sliced deep into its own poisonous tail.

> **To quickly grab another shard and use it to attack the creature's eye clusters, go to 8. To retreat while the creature tends to its wound, go to 11.**

13 You and Martha run at full pelt towards the warrior, yelling. Startled, he fails to raise his shield before Martha has planted an impressive karate kick in his midriff. As she dodges his retaliatory sword swipe, you dive into a kneeling position behind his legs. With a firm shove, Martha sends him toppling backwards over you to sprawl on the floor.

But just as you get the better of one of your enemies, the other is suddenly upon you.

'Look out!' you yell, as your alien assailant launches its lethal spear directly at Martha.

Martha ducks, and the spear narrowly misses. But it's allowed Martha's warrior opponent time to regain his feet and composure. You're back to one-on-one.

To retrieve the thrown spear and use it to attack your alien opponent, go to 8. To use the spear as a pole with which to vault the Arena wall, go to 57.

14 Downstairs is what appears to have been a kitchen area. But as above, it has been thoroughly ransacked. As you survey the mess, Martha appears in a doorway in the far wall.

'Ouch — somebody really went to town here!' she observes. 'Shame they've done such a job on the teleport.'

She nods to a booth in the corner of the room. A tangle of electrical cables spill from a smashed ceiling panel to dangle across its entrance, crackling and sparking dangerously, making it impossible to enter.

'Could've got where I want to be a lot faster via that — but I guess I'll have to do it the old-fashioned way!' She turns and hurries back out of the door.

You wonder if you could find something with which to push the hazardous cables aside, so that the teleport is usable.

To try your plan, go to 56. To follow Martha, go to 77.

15 | Accompanying the Doctor and Martha, you exit the cell block sector and emerge in a circular, domed area, full of equipment consoles. It appears to have been sabotaged – display screens have been smashed, and cables torn from their connections.

'Looks like the main communications area,' observes the Doctor. 'The convicts must have put it out of action during the breakout, to stop anyone calling for help.'

He scrutinizes a bundle of severed cables splaying from the back of a nearby device, then pulls out his sonic screwdriver.

'You two take a look around. I'll see if I can patch up a link with Group Nine HQ.'

As the Doctor sinks himself in his task, Martha heads for the room's other exit. You notice there is also a stairwell descending from the centre of the room.

To follow Martha, go to 77. To investigate the stairs, go to 18.

Your head swims sickeningly as you slowly regain consciousness. As your vision comes into focus, you become aware of a wild-eyed man with ruffled dark hair and long sideburns leaning over you, his face full of concern.

'Afraid you're going to feel as rough as a Sycorax's back end for a while. You've been out cold for over an hour. Would have felt a lot worse, mind you, if I hadn't turned up when I did and dealt with those charming friends of yours.'

He helps you sit up slowly.

'Where am I?' you ask, surveying the vast vault around you. It's like a giant cavern, ribbed with arched metal beams, and cluttered with makeshift electronics.

'You're in the TARDIS. To be more specific, you're in the TARDIS, on-board a Group Nine prisoner transport starship.'

The stranger fires a manic grin at you. 'Judging by your twenty-first-century fashion sense, though, I'm guessing the bigger surprise is when you are. It's the year...' — he crosses to consult a nearby console — '30506. How you come to be knocking about, beats me!'

'And who are you?'

The man extends a hand warmly, and pulls you to your feet.

'I'm the Doctor. Now, enough chat. We need to find Martha.'

You look blank.

The Doctor delves in the pocket of his pinstriped suit jacket and pulls out a crumpled photograph of an attractive young woman. 'My travelling companion,' he explains. 'She went to take a look around. Should have been back by now.'

He leads you down a ramp and through a double door, out of the TARDIS. To your utter bewilderment, you see that from outside, it appears to be nothing more than a modest-sized police phone box, standing in the centre of a narrow corridor.

'But...'

'Later,' says the Doctor. 'Now — which way, do you think?'

To follow the corridor left, go to 54. To go right, go to 87.

The teleport transports you to an identical booth in an entirely different location — a large, high-ceilinged hall, filled with noise, smells and bustle. Tables and benches hover, unsupported, throughout the area. Sitting at or slouched under the tables are around two hundred rowdy individuals. Few are human.

Despite being from many races, the crowd all share something in common — a brutish, hostile demeanour. Most are clutching vessels of thick green liquid, and look more than a little intoxicated.

You quickly duck under the nearest table — just as two alien thugs slump down at its far end.

"Nother fight tonight in the Arena. Big reckons he's got 'old of the Monorex of Grulg.'

'I've 'eard of him. From way back, isn't 'e?'

'S'right — fought off a Sycorax colonisin' force 'bout twenty millennia ago. Should be a good show.'

To continue listening, go to 92. To crawl across the hall under the tables, go to 81.

The stairs lead down into a lower section of the Communications Area. Here, too, the convict saboteurs have been busy. Crushed keyboards, smashed screens and twisted wiring are everywhere you look.

As you survey the damage, a figure suddenly hurries past the room's only doorway. It's Jal-Neth, presumably still working on disabling the Extraction Device.

You're about to follow him, to see if you can help, when you notice a small touchscreen in the otherwise featureless corridor wall directly opposite the exit. It shows a green button icon, with a single line of luminous text running below it:

EQUIPMENT TRANSIT: PRISONER EXERCISE AREA

As you touch the button out of curiosity, a previously invisible panel in the wall lifts and moves across, revealing an additional route.

To investigate the hidden door, go to 29.
To hurry after Jal-Neth, go to 37.

19 You sprint along the corridor, only to find yourself at what appears to be a dead end. There is, however, the opening of a ventilation shaft in one of the side walls — wide enough for a person to squeeze through.

Moments later, the Doctor joins you, breathless. He scans the featureless walls of the dead end, a look of concentration on his face. Then he moves purposefully to the end wall and pushes his arm straight through it.

'It's an illusion — some sort of projection. Should be able to walk through unharmed. Unless of course there's something nasty waiting on the other side…'

You hear the sound of heavy footsteps behind you.

The Doctor raises his thick eyebrows.

'Whaddya reckon — onwards…?' He nods to the vent, 'or upwards?'

To go through the fake wall, go to 91. To scramble up into the ventilation system, go to 63.

You square up to your vast alien foe, trying to anticipate whether it will attack first with its spear, claws or awesome fangs. But instead, the beast suddenly turns its body away from you, taking a vicious swipe at you with its club-like tail.

The massive tail swishes over your head, perilously close. Moments later it comes at you again, this time striking powerfully downwards. As you dodge to one side, its bulbous end crashes into the Arena floor, smashing through the surface. The watching convicts roar their appreciation.

The tail falls like a wrecking ball six more times. Each time you narrowly manage to evade it. Then, presumably tiring of pulverizing the Arena floor, the Monorex of Grulg turns back to face you.

To hurl some of the fragments of floor at your enemy, go to 30. To retreat, before the tail can strike again, go to 11.

21 You narrowly escape the danger, your escape route bringing you to a place where several corridors meet at a circular hub. A ladder rises through the floor, and continues through an opening in the ceiling.

You suddenly become aware of a peculiar noise. As it grows louder, something large begins to materialie beside the central ladder. It becomes ever more visible, until it stands before you, impossibly real — an old-fashioned, royal blue police telephone box.

The double doors of the box open and a man steps out. He looks about thirty-something, with tousled brown hair and hazel eyes, dressed in a pinstriped suit. He is closely followed by an attractive woman, ten or so years younger.

'So we know it's the year 30506, but you've no idea where the TARDIS has brought us, is that right Doctor?' asks the woman.

'Not entirely sure, Martha.' The man looks about enquiringly. 'Spaceship?' he offers tentatively. 'Human-built, I'd say.' He crosses to rap a knuckle on the glassy grey wall. 'Malthanite . . .' He looks pensive. 'Only used on Earth-built ships during the early thirtieth millennium ...' He moves to the ladder, scrutinising the motif on its rung treads — a pattern made of tiny number 9s. 'A-ha! Group Nine! Of course!' He turns back to Martha, triumphant. 'It's a prisoner transport vessel!'

'Well, let's take a look around,' says Martha, heading for the nearest corridor, still not having noticed you. The Doctor, however, has.

'Bless my cotton socks. Now that is interesting.' He murmurs, approaching. 'What's a twenty-first century kid like you doing in a thirtieth millennium spaceship like this?'

Before you can answer, a bolt of energy suddenly hits Martha in the chest, and she falls to the ground. The Doctor rushes to her aid, crouching to check her pulse.

'She's alive...'

He attempts to move her, but is driven back by a barrage of energy bolts. Armed alien figures are advancing along several of the corridors.

'Quick!' urges the Doctor. 'The ladder!'

To climb up, go to 53. To go down, go to 90.

---

22 You watch on the surveillance screen as the water sprinklers come on in the area below, drenching the surprised aliens. As the downpour continues, they hurriedly move off.

'That's those goons off our backs.' The Doctor quickly enters a sequence of commands on the touch screen that cause it to rapidly scan through area after area. 'Now let's see where they've taken Martha.'

Moments later, he has his answer. The display shows an image of Martha being bundled roughly into a cell. Her alien escorts take up sentry positions on either side of its door.

'Sector K45,' the Doctor reads from the display. 'Well – we can watch and wait...' A grin crosses his face as his eyes fall on the 'ALARM' command. 'Or we could try a little diversion...'

To keep watching on the monitor, go to 32. To set off the alarms in the neighbouring sector, go to 94.

23 You dive for the teleport booth, and Jal-Neth hurriedly taps its keypad. Instantly, you find yourself standing in an identical booth, in an entirely different location. It's packed with aisles of electronics cabinets, on the faces of which are thousands of green and red buttons, each pair bearing a coded label.

'Energy Control,' states Jal-Neth. 'If we can't get at the device itself, maybe we can knock out its power supply. I spotted the reference — it's on Line A8E5. Deactivate that, and we're in business.'

You split up to search for the correct power switch. But as you approach the end of the first aisle, you become aware of two convicts, weapons slung over their shoulders, standing a little way ahead. They have their backs to you, and are deep in conversation.

To attempt to sneak past, go to 9. To climb over the cabinets to the next aisle, go to 56.

24 You dash after the Doctor, aware that the newt-like alien is padding wetly after you. A blast of blue energy fizzes over your shoulder. Clearly he has a gun.

The Doctor dives to the right, and you follow, entering a lounge area scattered with low tables and stools.

As your pursuer bursts through the doorway and levels his weapon, the Doctor spins to face him, wild-eyed.

'OK, OK — don't shoot!'

The alien relaxes his trigger finger slightly.

'Just one request,' continues the Doctor, meekly. 'CATCH!'

Whipping his hand from a pocket, the Doctor tosses a small silver ball to the alien, who unthinkingly obeys his natural reactions, and catches it. Instantly his entire body goes rigid.

'Synaptic Disruptor,' explains the Doctor. 'Won't last long, so we'd better move.'

To take the room's other exit, go to 87.
To try the lift in the far wall, go to 47.

25 The Doctor leads you quickly away from the cells, passing through a pair of heavy-duty security doors that have been severely blast-damaged, into a complex of bunk rooms beyond. Here, mattresses are ripped, locker doors hang from their hinges and personal belongings are scattered everywhere.

'Crew quarters,' observes the Doctor, surveying the chaos in one typical bunk room. 'This'll be where the Group Nine officers slept. Looks like the whole area's been turned over by Big and his friends.'

In another bunk room, an amphibian-like convict sprawls on the bed, snoring, stone drunk.

The bunk rooms surround a communal lounge, also ransacked. In one corner, a stairwell leads to floors above and below.

'I wonder what we have up here…' ponders the Doctor, heading for the stairs.

To follow the Doctor up a floor, go to 79.
To investigate what lies down the stairs, go to 14.

Despite your efforts, your enemies quickly overpower you. You find yourself being shepherded along a series of passageways, until you come to an area where black doors line both sides of a wide corridor.

As a scar-faced guard taps in a code on a keypad beside one of the doors, it hisses open to reveal a prison cell, in which Martha is sitting glumly.

'You can spend some quality time with your friend 'ere,' smirks scar-face.

Suddenly, a figure in yellow and silver drops from the ceiling of the corridor, and attacks your guards. In a frenzy of expert martial arts moves, he quickly knocks two flat on their backs.

Hands freed by Martha, the Doctor whips a slim silver device from his pocket and uses it to unleash a sequence of blue energy bolts. The convicts turn and flee.

'Sonic screwdriver,' the Doctor informs you, with a wink, as he tucks the device away again.

'They'll be back,' says the uniformed man, watching the convicts retreat. He extends a hand to the Doctor.

'Jal-Neth, Group Nine.'

He quickly explains that he is one of the original crew of the prisoner transport ship you're on. It was on a routine mission to transfer a host of intergalactic criminals to a deep space penal colony, when there was a mass convict breakout, lead by Mr Big.

'Now Big has control of the ship, and he's using it for racketeering. He's developed a device that lets him extract famous warriors from different times and galaxies. Calls them his 'Tyrants of Time'. Forces them to fight one another, like gladiators. A whole host of low life turn up to see the show, and Big makes a killing on the gambling.'

The Doctor looks worried. 'Pulling key figures out of history will cause havoc to the Web of Time. The consequences could be catastrophic.'

'Not if we put a stop to it,' says Jal-Neth. 'I'll see what I can do about disabling the device, you figure out what we do next.'

He dashes off along the corridor.

To go with Jal-Neth, go to 37. To stick with the Doctor, go to 15.

The Doctor has yet to leave the cell block area. He appears to be having problems with his sonic screwdriver.

'Wretched thing's on the blink,' he explains, as you approach.

He scans the device across a blank section of the corridor wall, and its blue end flashes manically.

'It's giving off a reading for a concealed doorway here, and this' — he moves to a small numerical keypad a little further along the corridor wall — 'presumably opens it. But I can't get it to cooperate.'

He holds the screwdriver to the lock keypad, as on Martha's cell, but nothing happens.

'Never mind — best get a move on.' As the Doctor hurries away, it occurs to you to try the access code that Jal-Neth mentioned — 48713. You key it in. Sure enough, a doorway slides open in the previously blank wall.

To catch up with the Doctor, go to 79. To investigate what's through the revealed doorway, go to 29.

You descend, and find yourself in a laboratory. Its six walls are featureless but for its passageway and lift entrances.

The lab is dominated by a contraption very like the one via which you 'arrived', comprising a ring of vertical, fluid-filled tubes surrounding a circular platform. The device looks rather makeshift — some of the tubes have been repaired; wires are joined with temporary connectors; snipped cable ends and fluid-stained cloths litter the floor. You guess you are looking at an experimental prototype.

A bank of electronic displays stands beside the device. One shows a human face, under the heading 'EXTRACTION TARGET'. You recognise the man from a school project. It is Alexander the Great, the ancient Greek warrior.

As you accidentally brush a control screen, a red light flashes into life over the entrance passageway, and the lift's doors close abruptly.

To exit the laboratory, go to 38.
To continue looking around, turn to page 73.

The revealed exit leads to a small chamber. There is a transparent square set in the centre of its floor. You cross to investigate it. A fathomless vertical shaft falls away beneath your feet.

Without warning, four transparent panels spring up around you, a fifth dropping from above to seal you in a clear cubic prison. An instant later, the cube plummets into the unlit shaft below.

After a sickening fall, the cube suddenly decelerates, and is spat sideways from the blackness of the shaft into a brightly lit, wide open space. As your eyes adjust to the glare, you see that the cube is now standing alongside numerous others, at the edge of a circular walled arena. The other cubes hold menacing-looking warriors, mostly inhuman. All around you, tiers of makeshift seating are packed with onlooking convicts.

The walls of your cube suddenly dissolve away.

'Welcome to the Arena! This is an unexpected surprise!'

Mr Big is sitting at the heart of the unpleasant crowd.

'We were about to begin, with your charming friend here,' — Big gestures to Martha, who is standing a little way off — 'but I'm sure she'd be happy for you to join in the fun. You'll need a weapon, I suppose ...'

One of Big's associates slings something into the Arena beside you.

'Now — let me introduce you to two of our esteemed Tyrants of Time ...'

Big operates a hand-held remote, and two of the nearby transparent cubes dissolve. Out of the first, heading for Martha with a mad gleam in his eyes, strides a heavily-built Viking warrior.

A half-living, half-mechanical creature emerges from the second cube, riding a levitating platform. It is octopus-like, but much of its body has been technologically enhanced. Two of its numerous bionic limbs end in powerful robotic claws, while another terminates in a lethal laser-tipped dagger. The creature has its single 'eye' — a hi-tech lens grafted to its forehead — fixed firmly on you.

To pick up your 'weapon', go to 45. To run for it, go to 93.

30 You score a direct hit with one large piece of rubble, breaking off the bottom half of one of the Monorex's ferocious fangs. But this only serves to incense your enemy. He launches a frenzied attack, jabbing viciously at you with his spear and snarling in anger.

Retreating hastily, you seek the cover provided by the transparent prisoner cubes around the edge of the Arena. Your bulky opponent cannot move among these as quickly and easily as you, enabling you to keep one step ahead of its lethal tail strikes and spear jabs.

The jeering crowd is less than impressed with your evasive tactics, and a slow handclap builds in volume around the Arena.

To keep dodging among the prisoner cubes as a ploy to evade your enemy, go to 89. To make a break for the other side of the Arena, turn to page 59.

31 You dart along a random sequence of passageways in an attempt to shake off any followers.

Eventually, your route brings you to a wide corridor which opens into a huge, cathedral-sized hangar. You halt, breathless, and take in your remarkable surroundings. Several giant, turtle-shaped space vehicles stand unattended in docking bays on the hangar floor. The vast mouth of the hangar is sealed by some sort of shimmering energy field, through which you can see the starry void beyond.

A loading gantry spans the entire area, its service ladder leading to an exit high in the opposite wall. The only other way out seems to be a small door in the wall nearby.

The sound of running footsteps in the corridor behind you tells you that you haven't, after all, made your getaway.

To escape via the gantry ladder, turn to page 80. To try the small door, turn to page 74.

32 Your patience pays off. As you watch, Mr Big, accompanied by a pair of tough-looking alien heavies, suddenly approaches Martha's cell. One of the sentries opens it and drags Martha roughly from within.

'Delighted to make your acquaintance,' drawls Big, snidely. 'I'm most looking forward to your debut in the Arena. I must choose your opponent with care — Genghis Khan, perhaps?'

He abruptly snaps his fingers at one of his guards, who immediately enters the cell, and hauls a young man in a yellow and silver uniform from inside.

'I hope my young friend Jal-Neth has been good company. He's been a bit low since he and his pitiful Group Nine friends so spectacularly failed to prevent me and my fellow convicts from taking over this miserable hulk of a prison ship. Since then, of course, things have improved greatly. We now have the Arena on board, the greatest fight venue in history. You see, I've developed a device that allows me to choose my own gladiators — anyone, from any time. Imagine what people will pay to see Alexander the Great fight a tenth millennium Martian warlord!'

Big jabs a finger cruelly at Jal-Neth. 'But right now, it's this piece of dirt's turn.' He leers at Martha. 'You'll be soon...'

As Big and his guards escort Jal-Neth away along the corridor, the sentries lock Martha back in her cell, then follow.

As soon as they are gone, you hurry to Martha's cell. The Doctor pulls a slim silver device from his pocket.

'Sonic screwdriver,' he says, as if by explanation.

He touches the device on the lock keypad, and the door hisses open. Martha emerges, clearly delighted to see the Doctor.

The Doctor hurriedly introduces you, then gets back to business.

'If Big is pulling key people out of history, the consequences could be catastrophic. I need to find this device of his as quickly as possible.'

'OK, but I'm going after Jal-Neth,' insists Martha. 'He needs help.'

To accompany the Doctor, go to 25. To go with Martha, go to 77.

33 Your efforts prove futile — you are quickly apprehended. Your captors handle you roughly, dragging you along a number of corridors before bundling you through a doorway.

Mr Big is reclining in a stylish, ultra-modern chair behind a large levitating desk. He rises to approach you, sneering unpleasantly.

'How do you like my office? Formerly the residence of Group Nine's Chief Officer. But I'm afraid he no longer has any need of it...'

The small, spiteful man now stands right in front of you. 'Can you fight child, I wonder?' he spits at you. 'I do hope so, as you'll be making your debut in the Arena very shortly. Not alone, though — we have another volunteer...' You follow the dwarf's gaze. A man stands against one side wall, pinned against it by an electromagnetic shackle around his neck. He has dark hair, wild eyes, and is wearing a pinstriped suit.

'The Doctor here arrived shortly after you, in his ... what do you call that infernal blue box, Doctor?'

'The TARDIS,' snarls the shackled man, speech clearly hampered by the crackling blue band of energy looping across his throat. 'And it's a thousand-fold more sophisticated than anything you've got here in the thirtieth millennium.'

'I think not, Doctor,' sneers Mr Big. He crosses to activate a display screen in the wall. It shows an attractive young woman, slumped dejectedly on a grey bench, in a bare, cell-like room. 'But of course our opening act will be your young companion Martha.' He leers at the screen. 'Very pretty.'

While Big is preoccupied, you notice the Doctor discretely slip a silver device from his pocket and touch it to the energy shackle around his neck. The loop instantly expands, enabling the Doctor to duck his head through it. With a flick of the device, he casts the shackle at your guards, who suddenly find themselves entangled in writhing tendrils of fizzing blue energy.

'Come on!' the Doctor yells at you, dashing for the doorway. 'We've got to find Martha!'

To follow the Doctor, go to 43. To take the corridor in the opposite direction, go to 19.

34 You haven't gone far when you see a grey bed, like those in the cells, standing in the passageway a few metres ahead. As you approach it, there is a barely audible hiss behind you. You turn quickly to see a pair of gloss-black doors slice shut across the passage. The deathly silence that has so far hung over the prison cell corridors is shattered by an electronic voice.

'Solitary Confinement Cell G7 activated. All Prison Officers withdraw from proximity immediately. Cell will seal in 3... 2... 1...'

As a second pair of black doors begin to close a few metres further along the passageway, you have a split second to decide how to avoid imprisonment — should you shove the bed between the closing doors, or simply dive for the rapidly-vanishing gap?

To dive for the gap, go to 21. To jam the doors with the bed, go to 88.

35 | You descend to the floor of the canteen, and slip behind a trolley-like device floating nearby. On the nearest table, two gruff-looking yeti-like creatures are greedily scoffing from bowls of brown gloop.

As you peer around the trolley, you see a man in a ragged yellow and silver uniform approaching the table, carrying a jug of thick green liquid. He looks badly-beaten, and very nervous.

One of the yeti creatures cuffs the man around the head contemptuously.

''bout time, you lazy scum,' he growls. 'Bit different now we're in charge, isn't it? Mister la-di-dah Prison Officer.'

The man doesn't respond. Gathering up several empty jugs from the tabletop, he hurriedly places them on the levitating trolley, and steers it away to the next table — exposing you as he does so.

To dash for the canteen exit, go to 31. To bluff your way out of your predicament, go to 61.

36 | **W**ithin moments, two figures come thundering along the corridor. Watching from your hiding place, you see with alarm that neither is human. One is more or less humanoid, but for its stalked eyes. The other is huge, with matted grey fur all over its body, and three sloth-like claws on each limb. Both are carrying hi-tech firearms.

As Stalk-Eyes scans the area, Fur-Face produces what looks disturbingly like a real human eye, and holds it up to the retinal scanner. The alarm ceases.

'Personnel match successful, Prison Officer Kel-Hoon. Access authorised.'

The doors slide open, and the two creatures rush inside. Minutes later, presumably having searched the area within, they re-emerge. They confer, in a series of grunts, with their backs to you. You seize your chance to slip silently past and through the doors.

Immediately inside, the passageway slopes down, branching into two.

To head left, go to 75. To go right, go to 28.

You hurry after Jal-Neth along a series of deserted passageways until you come to the room where you first arrived. At its centre stands the Extraction Device that brought you to this distant time and place, its fluid-filled tubes bubbling gently.

There's no sign of the orange grasshopper creature you encountered earlier. Happy that the coast is clear, Jal-Neth crosses to examine the Extraction Device.

'We need to find some way to deactivate it, but without putting it permanently out of action,' he mutters. 'We might still need to adapt it to get you and the rest of Big's time travelling warriors back where you belong.'

He gestures to a cubicle on the far wall.

'Watch the teleport, and the door, in case we get company…'

Even as he speaks, you hear approaching footsteps in the corridor outside.

To quickly hide, go to 39. To escape via the teleport, go to 23.

38 As you head for the exit, a thick transparent shield suddenly drops across it, sealing it completely. You hastily try the lift instead, but its doors are tightly sealed, too. Your heart sinks as you turn back to the transparent door barrier, only to see a pair of lizard-like aliens now crouched behind it, leering at you.

A moment later, you understand why they haven't entered the room. Small clouds of bright yellow gas are blossoming from hissing outlets in the ceiling. As some of the vapour finds its way into your lungs, you feel an instant wooziness.

Looking up at the gas outlets, you notice the opening of a ventilation duct in the ceiling. Standing on one of the equipment consoles, you may be able to reach it.

To hold your breath and try to force the lift doors, go to 16. To clamber into the ventilation duct, go to 21.

39 From your hiding place crouched behind a stack of cylindrical silver canisters, you see the orange grasshopper-like creature scuttle into the room. It is accompanied by a second alien, heavily-built and reptilian.

'Ve must make ready ze seestom for a furzer extraction zees night,' Grasshopper tells his companion, moving towards the Extraction Device's control console. 'Attila, brutal champion of ze Huns.'

Jal-Neth is curled up behind the console. You can see that he is about to be discovered.

'Look out!'

Your warning yell gives Jal-Neth the element of surprise. He bursts past the startled aliens, out of the doorway through which you entered. As the grasshopper creature gives chase, the other alien turns its attention to you, its yellow slit-eyes filled with menace.

To make a break for the room's other exit, go to 51. To fend off the creature by throwing canisters at it, go to 9.

You hurry up the steps to find the Doctor engrossed in a giant, ultra-thin display screen hovering impossibly at the centre of the mezzanine.

'Fabulous device,' he murmurs, without averting his gaze. 'Has a primitive psychic interface. You simply choose command options clearly in your mind…'

You watch as the Doctor frowns slightly with concentration, and a sequence of control menus flash past at lightning speed on the screen.

'Here we are — cell sectors…'

At that moment, you see three figures burst through the doorway below. Spotting you, they rush for the stairs.

'Doctor!'

The Doctor breaks off from the screen and turns to face the trio of rough-looking aliens now advancing menacingly.

'You get out of here!' urges the Doctor. 'I'll hold them off!'

To leap from the mezzanine, and escape via the narrow corridor, go to 19. To stand and fight alongside the Doctor, go to 26.

After a short distance, the corridor opens out on one side to form a balcony. Sounds of noisy revelry come from below.

As you cross to the balcony's edge, you find yourself overlooking a large, busy dining area. It is packed with peculiar creatures — over two hundred, you guess — eating and drinking at long, levitating tables. You spot a handful of humans, but the vast majority of the rowdy crowd are unlike any beings you've seen before, a menagerie of furry, scaly, multi-limbed and multi-eyed monsters.

The corridor continues ahead of you. At the far end of the balcony, a spiral staircase descends to the canteen.

Considering the freakish and rough-looking demeanour of the diners, you're tempted to keep going. But by moving closer, to eavesdrop, you might pick up some information to help make sense of your bizarre situation.

To continue along the corridor, go to 71.
To take the steps down to the canteen, go to 35.

You and Martha catch up with Jal-Neth in a circular, domed area, full of equipment consoles. He is busy at one of them.

'Main Communications Area,' Jal-Neth states, without looking up. 'Thought I'd try to send out a Mayday signal to headquarters, but Big must have changed the Systems Access Code. It used to be 48713, but that's not working.'

He bangs a fist down angrily on the console top as the computer once again refuses to let him log on.

'OK. Maybe I can find Big with his dratted Extraction Device. I'll soon get the new codes out of him ...'

And he hurries away along one of the exit corridors.

'I'll keep trying,' says Martha, taking his place at the control console. 'See if I can find a way to set up a signal.'

To follow Jal-Neth, go to 37. To go back and rejoin the Doctor, go to 27.

43 You follow the Doctor as he ducks into a doorway on the corridor's left, and find yourself in a large computer-filled room. A central spiral stairway swirls up to a mezzanine floor above, crowded with yet more technical equipment.

'We need to dig up something that'll help us find our way around,' says the Doctor, urgently. 'Martha must be in some sort of confinement area. Maybe we can find out where. I'll take upstairs, you have a look around down here.'

Most of the displays are filled with technical read-outs, or information in system code that is gobbledygook to you. You can't find anything that gives a clue to Martha's whereabouts.

A narrow corridor leads from the back of the room, presumably to an adjoining area.

To take the corridor to continue your search, go to 86. To join the Doctor on the gallery, go to 40.

As you run for your life, you become separated from the Doctor. Moments later, one of your pursuers brings you down in a crunching tackle. Within minutes, you are being roughly escorted into a cell block area.

'In there, you little scumbag,' orders your unpleasant captor, shoving you into a cell and locking the door behind you.

The cell is bare but for a bench-like bed, on which is sitting an intelligent-faced man in a tattered yellow and silver uniform.

The man introduces himself as Jal-Neth, a Group Nine prison guard. He explains that the ship you are on — a prisoner transporter called the S.S. Custodian — has been taken over by its convict inmates, after a mass breakout led by Mr Big.

'And now Big's set up this prize-fighting racket,' continues Jal-Neth. 'He's developed some sort of device that lets him extract individuals from history — guess that's how you got here. He's using it to pick legendary warriors to fight one another. 'Tyrants of Time', he calls them.'

Your conversation is interrupted as the cell door suddenly hisses open. The Doctor stands outside, Martha at his side, and a slim silver cylinder in his hand.

'Sonic screwdriver,' grins the Doctor. 'Marvellous for locks!'

You hurry away from the cell together. As you do so, you quickly relay what Jal-Neth has told you.

'That's bad,' says the Doctor. 'Very bad. If Big really is extracting key historical figures, there'll be disastrous repercussions.'

As you meet an intersecting corridor, Jal-Neth halts abruptly.

'I need to get to Communications. See if I can contact HQ.' He darts away down the left-hand passage.

The Doctor turns to Martha, and points straight on. 'You go that way — check on the TARDIS. I'll see what I can do about this Extraction Device.' Then he turns, and hurries away down the right-hand corridor.

To go with Martha, go to 77. To accompany the Doctor, go to 25.

The 'weapon' Big has provided appears to be a pair of heavy metal balls joined by a length of thin wire. You suddenly realize what it is — a futuristic version of a bolus, an ancient throwing weapon.

As your opponent comes swooping closer on its hovering platform, mechanical pincers snapping ferociously, you hurriedly grab the weapon and attempt to use it. Holding the centre of the wire, you swing the bolus balls in a wide circle over your head, then launch them at the oncoming monster.

For a first-timer, your aim is superb. The wire part of the bolus wraps itself tightly around several of the creature's multiple limbs, leaving them immovable. The beast brings its attack platform to a standstill, struggling to free its ensnared arms.

To knock the creature down, while it is still entangled, go to 60. To get as far from it as possible, go to 46.

46 | As you retreat, you stumble over a wooden shield on the Arena floor. It has been discarded by Martha's opponent, who is using both hands to grapple with her nearby.

Despite your evasive efforts, your enemy stalks you doggedly, impossible to shake off. Its single inhuman eye is focused intensely on your every move, as it waits for the ideal moment to attack.

It occurs to you that if you could cover this awful eye, you'd stand some chance against the creature. You hastily remove your jacket, and as the creature bears down upon you, you fling it over its face and dodge away. The monster snarls in frustration, and awkwardly sets about tearing away the obstruction to its vision.

> **To sprint to the other side of the Arena while your enemy can't see, go to 76. To seize your chance to grab the discarded shield, go to 99.**

47 | As you step from the lift, it closes silently behind you. You're in a wide corridor, lined with tall, grey lockers.

Each bears a name, serial number and a silver and yellow '9' logo.

The Doctor opens the nearest locker, labelled 'Zhang — PO552491', and removes a hi-tech firearm. He examines it briefly, then, to your alarm, takes aim at you and pulls the trigger.

Nothing happens.

'Fingerprint sensitive,' grins the Doctor. 'Only our friend Mr Zhang can fire this. Standard protection on all Group Nine weaponry.'

'And child's play to override,' sneers a familiar voice. You turn to see Mr Big, standing in the open lift. He is flanked by two aliens, both holding weapons like the one you've been looking at.

The Doctor gives you an anxious glance, and silently mouths the word 'run'.

To make a break to your left, with the Doctor, go to 44. To flee in the opposite direction, alone, go to 86.

48 As you back away from the ladder, the first of your pursuers drops to the floor. He is armed with a pistol-like weapon.

'Plasma blaster! Take cover!' yells the Doctor, bundling you behind one of the stacks of tiles as the alien opens fire. A bolt of crackling green energy hits a tile only inches from your head. Its dark surface absorbs the blast, leaving it undamaged.

The Doctor thrusts another Dissipation Cell at you. 'They'll work as shields!'

Two more aliens have now joined the first. As they advance, firing, you and the Doctor struggle to block the lethal plasma bolts.

'Not sure we can hold them off!' the Doctor yells, amid the barrage. Your assailants move to block the exit doorway. 'But we might make it back up the ladder...'

To stand your ground, go to 26. To dash for the ladder and scramble to its top, go to 53.

49 The area you've entered comprises two rooms — one a full-blown surgical theatre, the other a general treatment room. This has a second exit. As its doors on to the corridor outside suddenly open, you dive for cover behind a treatment table.

From your hiding place, you watch two alien thugs guide a hi-tech floating stretcher through the doorway. A human lies unconscious on it. He is dressed like a Roman centurion. Across his chest are three horrific gashes, as though he has been gored by a terrible claw.

'Soon patch 'im up and get 'im back in the Arena,' smirks the first alien.

'S'right,' agrees his partner. 'Big wants 'is money's worth, after all.'

The pair chuckle cruelly, and set about configuring one of the room's robotic devices to tend to the Roman's wounds.

To attempt to stay hidden, go to 9. To slip quietly into the corridor when you get a chance, go to 51.

As you follow the glassy grey corridor further, it leads to a square, low-ceilinged room. Six cubicle-like booths stand against one wall. On the opposite wall is a large video screen, displaying some sort of layout-plan, beneath the heading S.S. Custodian.

A hulking, inhuman figure, with lumpy green skin and pig-like eyes and snout, is contemplating the display, swaying slightly. Giving a mighty belch, the alien touches part of the plan on the screen, which blinks in response. An electronic voice speaks silkily:

'You have selected the Staff Canteen area. Please enter Teleport 3.'

The alien totters into the third booth. Turning, he sees you for the first time. His piggy eyes narrow in drunken puzzlement, then a pulse of blue light suddenly illuminates the floor and walls of the cubicle, and he vanishes altogether.

To use the teleport yourself, go to 17. To explore the layout-plan, go to 67.

51 You hurry along the corridor, which gradually descends, until you suddenly emerge in a wide open space, surrounded by a circular wall. Spotlights in the high, domed ceiling illuminate the central area. Distributed around its perimeter are dozens of large transparent cubes. And at its centre stands Martha, alone.

Tiers of makeshift seats rise on all sides. Hundreds of convicts are busy settling into them, as though for a show. You spy the diminutive Mr Big among them.

Mr Big meets your gaze, and leers. He touches a device on his wrist, and the doorway through which you entered is immediately sealed.

'This is a most pleasant surprise,' sneers Big. 'Welcome to the Arena, the number one fight venue in this, or any other galaxy! Our first contest this evening was to have been between your good friend here and our current human champion, Genghis Khan. But now you can tackle another of our 'Tyrants of Time' alongside her — the legendary Monorex of Grulg, perhaps?'

Big gestures to one of the transparent cubes. A terrifying hulk lurks within it. His body is covered in thick hoops of scaly armour, like an armadillo's. He has a thick, muscular tail, ending in a viciously spiked club-like lump. In one of his clawed forelimbs he is clutching a long bone spear. His face is the stuff of nightmares — three-eyed and hideously fanged.

You now see that the other cubes contain figures, too — ferocious-looking individuals of many different species.

Mr Big addresses the assembled throng gleefully.

'Let the contest begin!'

He operates his wristband remote again, and the walls of two of the transparent cubes dissolve. The freed Monorex lumbers towards you, hissing, while the tough-looking Mongolian warrior released from the other cube makes a beeline for Martha.

To stand your ground, go to 20. To run for it, go to 59.

The giant grasshopper continues to approach, muttering to itself.

'Eet should have verked. I verified ze chronological coordinates. Zees Earthling should be Alexander ze Great. Legendary human vorrier. Ve must delete and re-extract...'

As the creature draws near, you attempt to reason with it. But before you can say a word, it lunges at you with the cattle prod device. You dodge to one side, and the creature stumbles, off-balance.

The pulsing end of the prod makes contact with one of the fluid-filled tubes, sending a fizzling blue network of energy up the grasshopper's arm and across its alien body. As the sparks subside, the creature crumples to the floor, unconscious.

Looking around in panic, you see a second exit at the opposite side of the room. It opens into a corridor with grey, glass-like walls, seemingly deserted.

To follow the corridor left, go to 41. To go right, go to 95.

53 You emerge through a hatch in the floor of a circular room. The Doctor quickly closes and locks it to prevent anyone following you. There is no other exit.

The walls are lined with dozens of video screens, showing various areas of the spaceship. Each display incorporates a control menu, with 'LIGHTING ON/OFF', 'FIRE' and 'TEMP +/−' among the commands. You are clearly in some sort of surveillance and control centre.

One screen shows a corridor, along which Martha's unconscious body is now being dragged by a pair of alien thugs. Another shows the area directly below you. You can see several figures milling around the TARDIS.

'We need to get past them to help Martha,' states the Doctor. 'We could kill the lights, or perhaps set off the sprinklers — what do you think?'

To trigger the anti-fire sprinklers, go to 22. To turn off the area's lighting, go to 7.

After a short distance the corridor joins several others at a circular hub. In the centre of the junction, a ladder rises through an opening in the ceiling.

You can just make out the sound of receding footsteps, and the faint cries of a female voice protesting. But as the sounds echo along the converging passageways, it is impossible to tell which corridor they are coming from.

There are signs of a recent scuffle — a jacket with one sleeve almost torn off lies discarded on the floor, alongside several handfuls of green fur.

'Martha's,' says the Doctor, frowning. 'The jacket — not the fur,' he clarifies, as he stoops to pick it up. Beneath the jacket, a device rather like a mobile phone lies on the floor.

To investigate where the ladder leads, go to 53. To take a closer look at the phone-like device, go to 4.

55 You clamber onto the elevated walkway and follow it across towards the opening in the wall ahead. But as you move nearer, you realise that the walkway doesn't actually reach it. There is a gap of about four metres — too far to jump — between the end of the walkway and the opening in the wall.

The very end of the walkway looks like it is designed to extend telescopically. There is a green button on the wall next to the doorway ahead.

You wonder if by hitting the button with something, you might be able to trigger the walkway to extend to the door.

Your other option is to return to the lift and try the 'CLASSIFIED' button.

You can hear the lizard creatures returning — it's time to make yourself scarce.

To throw your shoe at the button, go to 88. To hurry back to the lift, go to 28.

56 Before you can put your plan into action, you feel a sudden sting on the back of your neck. You reach up and pluck a tiny needle-tipped dart from your skin. Turning, you see a silver globe, with a single eye-like lens, hovering just behind you. Moments later, everything goes black.

When you regain consciousness, you find yourself lying face down on an unfamiliar floor. A deafening din of jeering voices fills your throbbing head. As you struggle to your feet, you see that a crowd of inhuman-looking spectators is gathered all around in staggered rows. You are standing at the centre of a makeshift amphitheatre.

'Welcome to the Arena, my young friend!' Mr Big is seated in a prominent position among the crowd. 'So glad you've woken up at last. Your friend here is itching to get underway.'

As Big gives a callous laugh, you follow his gaze to see Martha standing nearby.

'All bets placed? Then release the Tyrants of Time!'

At Big's signal, the aliens on either side of him clamber down on to two large transparent cubes standing at the edge of the Arena. Inside the first, a grotesque figure is stomping and snorting angrily. It is monstrously sabre-toothed, with a crown of lethal head spikes. But more striking by far is its single giant compound eye. This fly-eyed Cyclops is clad in crystalline armour, and is carrying a long, thin, laser-tipped fighting staff.

The second cube holds a tough-looking human warrior in the battle dress of Ancient Greece. Other imposing-looking fighters are similarly imprisoned in other cubes all around the Arena's perimeter.

The front panels of the two cubes suddenly dissolve. As the Grecian warrior strides aggressively towards Martha, the bug-eyed monster comes charging straight for you.

To look around for something to fight with, go to 69. To run for it, go to 46.

You manage to clear the Arena wall — but only to find yourself in the midst of the angry convict crowd.

An evil-looking humanoid with a pincer-tipped bionic arm bears down on you, his claw twitching menacingly. Other murderous-looking convicts close in on all sides.

Then, suddenly, every one of your would-be assailants crumples to the floor. The crowd falls silent, as every convict in it slumps down, out cold. Only the warriors within the Arena remain conscious.

'Knockout!'

You turn to see the Doctor, beaming, making his way towards you through the piles of prone bodies.

'But how …?' you stammer.

The Doctor crouches beside the pincer-armed convict and lifts his shaggy mane to reveal the back of his neck. There is a small metallic disc, with the Group Nine logo on it, embedded in the convict's skin.

'Neural Inhibitor,' explains the Doctor. 'Group Nine surgically implant all Class A prisoners with one. It can be remotely triggered to deliver a powerful neural impulse — enough to knock you out — if a prisoner gets too frisky. Can't be removed without causing coma. They're meant to be activated simultaneously if there's an uprising. Mr Big must have deleted the trigger code from the ship's security systems before he led the break out. I just needed a while to figure out what the code was, then —' the Doctor gestures to the unconscious criminals. 'Night-night!'

Martha and Jal-Neth, armed, now join you. 'He gave me a helping hand back there,' Martha gestures to the Arena. 'What now?'

'You two get this lot tucked up snug in their cells,' says the Doctor. He drapes his arm around your shoulders. 'We'll go and see what we can do about reversing Mr Big's Extraction Device. It's time we got our young friend here — plus Napoleon, Genghis and all the rest — back where they belong!'

As the Doctor strides off purposefully, you accompany him, glad that your ordeal in the Arena is over. Glad to be going home.

This adventure in time and space is over.

The lift opens onto a huge chamber, the size of an aircraft hangar. It is dominated by a pair of colossal, grey spheres, connected by a wide cylindrical channel with thick transparent walls. A flickering arc of blue light burns fiercely within the transparent tube. You guess this immense device is some kind of power-generating equipment.

A reptilian alien stands beside an empty booth at the foot of the giant reactor. As you watch, a second creature suddenly materialises out of thin air in the booth beside him. Stepping out, it engages the first creature in hissing conversation. They move off together, away from where you watch, unnoticed.

Apart from the lift and teleport booth, the only route out of this Engineering area appears to be via an elevated walkway that leads to a door midway up the far wall.

To use the teleport, go to 17. To take the walkway, go to 55.

You head for the centre of the Arena, seeking to stay well beyond your terrible adversary's reach. You are joined there by a breathless Martha.

'I don't fancy yours much,' she gasps, with a strained grin.

As your alien opponent lumbers closer, so too, from the other direction, does the ancient human warrior against whom Martha has been pitted. He is brandishing his sword wildly, eyes glazed with a psychotic expression.

'Yours looks like a real pussycat,' you reply, grimly.

'What about if we double-up?' suggests Martha. 'We could both try to concentrate an attack on one of them, then tackle the other.'

'It's worth a try,' you agree.

'OK — who's first?'

To take on your alien adversary together, go to 96. To tackle Martha's human opponent first, go to 13.

Your body charge is sufficient to ram the octopus-like creature's levitating platform into the Arena wall. The platform tilts dramatically on impact, causing the alien creature to tumble awkwardly to the floor. Then the platform stabilizes, remaining levitating against the wall, at about your waist height.

The creature lets out an ear-splitting screech of anger. Its multiple mechanically-enhanced limbs thrash violently, as it strives to right itself on the floor. Despite being less mobile now that it is off its special platform, it is nevertheless still utterly deadly. Thoroughly maddened, its pincers snap frenziedly at you, its laser dagger slashing wildly.

As the crowd sense the creature's increased aggression, they roar their appreciation, egging it on.

To retreat before the creature has time to regain its levitating platform, go to 93. To make use of the platform yourself, to scale the Arena wall, go to 57.

61 You rise slowly, doing your very best to look casual. The two brutish aliens on the nearest table are staring at you suspiciously.

'Who're you?' grunts one, "N whaddya up to?'

Pulse racing, you explain, in your gruffest voice, that Mr Big has sent you to the canteen on a private errand – to fetch him some food and drink. You were just trying to find what he wanted on the trolley.

'Mr Big? Hmph.' The larger alien looks a little uncertain. 'Best get a move on then, 'adn't ya, or you'll be next on the bill for the Arena.'

His companion gives a gruff laugh. To your immense relief, both creatures turn back to their food, no longer interested in you.

To keep up the bluff, and stroll casually to the canteen exit, go to 21. To hurry back up the balcony steps, and continue along the corridor, go to 71.

The Doctor calls up data on a number of other unlikely inmates — from a Roman centurion to a two-hundredth-millennium bear-like warrior from the planet Athox — until an image of Martha suddenly appears on the screen.

'Cell 17 — let's go ...'

You follow the Doctor to a junction in the corridor. As you crouch down and peer cautiously around the corner, you can see a door marked 17 — closely guarded by a pair of tough-looking aliens, weapons in hand.

'Plasma pistols,' whispers the Doctor. 'Not to be messed with. I guess we'll have to sit it out.'

You notice the cell door opposite, through the window of which you can see the bear-like creature from Athox. It occurs to you that an escaped prisoner might just divert the attention of Martha's guards.

To stay hidden, and wait, go to 32.
To release the bear-like prisoner as a diversion, go to 94.

63 After a lot of crawling and squirming, you and the Doctor find your way through a series of ventilation shafts to another opening. The Doctor inches cautiously forward to take a peek. Moments later he shuffles back to whisper to you.

'Jackpot! We've come out in one of the cell block corridors, near where they're holding Martha. Looks like she's got a couple of heavies keeping an eye on her, though.'

The Doctor does some awkward wriggling, attempting to take something from his jacket pocket. Finally, he produces what appears to be a blank sheet of paper.

'This might do the trick. Psychic paper. I should be able to make them think they've got orders to attend an emergency elsewhere.'

To drop down into the corridor, for the Doctor to try his diversion tactic, go to 94. To stay hidden, and watch for a chance to release Martha, go to 32.

64 The display reverts to the layout diagram. You notice several icons down its edge. As you touch one labelled 'Convict Status', several hundred orange dots appear, widely scattered across the map. The biggest cluster by far appears in the area labelled 'Staff Canteen'. Some are moving along corridors. None appear within the 'Cell blocks' area.

You try another icon, labelled 'Secure'. It changes colour. When nothing else happens, you touch the 'Internal Teleport Bay' section of the map again. Instantly, there is a fizz of electrical energy on either side of you as a shimmering, translucent-blue sheet seals each of the room's exit corridors. On the screen, a flashing alert appears:

STUN-SHIELDS ACTIVE: AREA SECURE

The screen goes blank. You appear to have trapped yourself. To make matters worse, you can hear the approach of running footsteps.

To attempt to pass either stun-shield, go to 16. To try the teleport, go to 17.

The gigantic creature scuttles closer, then launches a fierce attack with its huge, razor-sharp claws, striking at you with first one, then the other. You do your best to fend off the deadly pincers with your shield, but each time you do so, the creature's claws crush and splinter the timber.

Suddenly the barrage ceases. The beast retracts its claws and elevates its rear end. An instant later, the venomous, barbed end of its tail whips down at you from above.

You just manage to block the lethal sting with your damaged shield, but the force of the attack sends you sprawling. There's a roar of delight from the watching crowd.

You scramble back to your feet as the creature comes at you again.

To hurl the remains of your shield at the creature, and run, go to 93. To try to get behind it, so it can't strike at you, go to 12.

66 You make it out of the doorway, into a narrow corridor that runs in both directions. To your right, you can see Mr Big walking away, muttering angrily, so you hurriedly head in the opposite direction. To your relief, there is no sign that the grasshopper creature is coming after you.

As you follow the passageway, you take in your strange surroundings. The grey walls, floor and ceiling of the corridor are made of a material you've never seen before — something opaque and glass-like. There is no visible lighting, yet the corridor is somehow brightly illuminated.

You come to a place where a short stretch of one wall is transparent. As you lean against it to peer through, the area around your right palm glows warm red, and the section of wall slides silently sideways to create an opening.

To enter the doorway, go to 82. To continue along the corridor, go to 50.

67 The giant screen seems comparatively straightforward. There's a main diagram, rather like a floor plan or blueprint, on which different areas are labelled. Some labels are self-explanatory — 'Staff Canteen', 'Prisoner Exercise Area', 'Washroom' — while others, such as the 'E-Flux Outlet', are less familiar.

You find a small section of the diagram labelled 'Internal Teleport Bay', and touch it experimentally with your index finger. The display instantly changes into a larger scale, photo-real image of the area you are currently standing in.

To your puzzlement, the image shows a corridor continuing from the room's far wall, which in reality appears to be doorless. But as you tentatively touch this missing corridor on the display, the central section of the seemingly solid wall beside you splits open, revealing the mystery corridor beyond.

To take a look along the revealed corridor, go to 71. To continue using the touchscreen, go to 64.

68 A helter-skelter chute ride deposits you in a room filled entirely with plastic rubbish. Floundering amid the junk, you take a look around. The only exit is a sealed hatch in one end wall.

Suddenly, there is a low mechanical growl, and the side walls begin to inch inwards. You are in a rubbish compacter. If you don't get out quickly, you'll be crushed with the plastic bottles.

You hurriedly try the hatch. When it won't budge, you take your only remaining option — hammer wildly on it and scream for help.

At the last moment, the hatch swings open. From the corridor outside, the Doctor helps you scramble out of the now uncomfortably narrow jaws of the compacter.

Unfortunately, the Doctor isn't the only one to have heard your cries. Three alien convicts come hurrying around the corner.

To take on the convicts, go to 26. To run for it, go to 44.

69 You spot something on the Arena floor not far from where you are standing, and hurry to investigate. You're in luck — it's an ancient-looking shortsword, presumably left there by a previous — all-too-likely deceased — Arena contestant.

As your monstrous opponent bears down on you, you eagerly snatch up the weapon and thrust it fiercely at its alien body. The creature effortlessly parries your repeated jabs with its own hi-tech fighting staff.

Deciding that close combat isn't such a good idea, you quickly back off, then launch your weapon javelin-like at the creature's hideous single eye.

But your aim is wide of the mark. The sword is deflected harmlessly by the monster's crystalline body armour, and you are once more left weaponless.

To retreat as fast as you can, go to 59. To attempt to recover the sword, go to 10.

The doors to the Cryogenic Vault hiss open, then close again behind you. The Vault holds a dozen transparent, coffin-like pods, each connected by a network of tubes and wires to banks of complex monitoring equipment.

Two of the pods hold patients, presumably frozen by Group Nine medical staff before the prisoner breakout. One holds a young woman, whose appearance gives no clue to her ailment. A badly burnt man lies frozen in the second pod.

Suddenly, you hear sounds of a scuffle, and the Doctor's protests, coming from the adjoining Medical Bay. The sound of approaching footsteps follows.

You wonder if you could somehow quickly block the entrance to the Vault — or perhaps pose as a patient by climbing into one of the unoccupied cryogenic pods…

To smash the door-lock keypad in the hope that it will disable the doors, go to 9. To try your deception plan, go to 56.

After several minutes walking, you reach what remains of a pair of heavy silver doors standing across the corridor. A large jagged opening has been torn in them, presumably by an explosive blast. You clamber through.

Beyond the wrecked doors, the corridor widens. At regular intervals along either wall stand square, gloss-black slabs, each with a small transparent window at its centre. You peer through the window of the first slab, and realise that it is actually a door. Beyond it, you can see what is clearly a prison cell, bare but for a pair of grey benches — presumably beds.

The next dozen or so cells are also unoccupied. Beyond the seventh cell on the left, a narrow passageway branches off the main corridor. Ahead, more cell doors line both walls of the corridor.

To take the passageway on the left, go to 34. To carry straight on, go to 98.

Your efforts are in vain. Defeated, you await your opponent's decisive blow.

But an instant later, the monster vanishes. There is a roar of dismay from the watching crowd.

As you scan the Arena, bewildered, it's clear that all the warriors — including Martha's opponent and those in the transparent cubes — have disappeared into thin air.

The doors of the Arena entrance tunnel suddenly open, and a host of heavily-armed troops in yellow and silver uniforms pour into the Arena, led by Jal-Neth. Stun-guns blazing, they quickly begin to round up the crowd of surprised convicts.

From amid the chaos, the Doctor comes striding towards you, smirking.

'Had him just where you wanted him, huh?'

'But ... where did they all go?'

'Back to where they came from. I guessed Big's device might be fairly primitive. When it extracts someone from time, there's a residual temporal link that acts to pull them back. Like they're still attached to their own time with elastic. Instead of properly severing the links — which takes some tricky temporal dynamics — the device simply overrode the pull, by drawing power from the ship's reactor. Crude, but effective. All I had to do was divert the power for a split second and — twang! — everyone gets yanked back into their original existence.'

'And the Group Nine guards?' asks Martha, who has joined you.

'Jal-Neth managed to patch up external communications and reactivate the Teleport Bay. Called up reinforcements.' The Doctor surveys the battle raging around the Arena. 'I think we can safely leave them to see Big and co. back behind bars.'

You're still puzzled. 'But why didn't I disappear?'

The Doctor puts his arm around your shoulders. 'I personally severed your temporal link, my friend. Thought you might prefer to return to the twenty-first century by TARDIS. How about it?'

You answer with a wide grin, then head off with the Doctor and Martha to the exit of the Arena.

This adventure in time and space is over.

As you continue exploring the laboratory, you find details of several more 'extraction targets' on documents scattered on a messy desktop. But in these instances the individuals are not only unfamiliar — they are not even human. There is one thing they all have in common, though — awesome, warrior-like physiques.

Suddenly, a gruff voice speaks from behind you.

'Turn around slowly, squirt.'

You turn to see a heavily-built man, extensively tattooed, standing in the doorway to the lab. He has a hi-tech handgun trained on you. A knee-high, rat-faced creature is skulking just behind him, sneering at you nastily.

'Mr Big'll want to speak to you. Don't try anything smart — this is set to stun, but I can soon change that.'

He gestures for you to move into the corridor.

To make a break past him, go to 16.
To knock the gun from his grasp, then grapple with him, go to 33.

The door leads into a washroom. There are hi-tech hand basins, toilet cubicles and a large communal shower area. A touchscreen beside the shower bay includes a glowing ON/OFF icon, plus additional controls for its sophisticated system of water jets.

Hearing the door hiss open behind you, you dive for cover into one of the cubicles. As you enter, a wide beam of red light tracks across your body. An instant later the toilet's height and seat shape automatically adjust for a perfect fit. Cool loo!

The two alien creatures that have been following you are now searching the washroom. Peering from the cubicle, you can see them checking the shower area. It occurs to you that by giving them a drenching, you might be able to create enough confusion to make a getaway.

To turn on the showers as a diversion, go to 88. To attempt to sneak out unnoticed, go to 33.

The passage leads to a large storeroom. Translucent vertical screens divide the area into aisles. Mounted on the screens are row upon row of close combat weapons.

One aisle holds a remarkable range of swords. Some you recognise from history lessons: a hefty antique broadsword; a curving Samurai blade. Others are extraordinary: a triple-bladed weapon with a hilt so large no human could wield it; another with a slim, flexible filament for a blade, its hilt studded with electronic controls.

You carefully take down this last weapon. As you swish it from side to side experimentally, the blade's entire length is suddenly engulfed in green flames. It slices effortlessly through part of the solid screen.

A loud grunt makes you spin round. Fur-Face and Stalk-Eyes are moving menacingly towards you from the armoury's entrance.

> **To drop the weapon and dash for the room's other exit, go to 31. To stand and fight, go to 33.**

At the edge of the Arena stand more of the transparent cubes in which Big's gruesome 'Tyrants of Time' are caged, ready for battle. As you run towards them, desperate to get away from your monstrous one-eyed adversary, it occurs to you that even if you somehow manage to survive your present encounter, Mr Big may simply release another of these horrors to finish you off.

From the other side of the Arena, you can hear the grunts, shrieks and yells arising from Martha's encounter with her awesome opponent. She is clearly putting up a brave fight. But eventually for her, as for you, survival seems all but impossible.

To use the cubes to evade your opponent, dodging for cover behind and between them, go to 89. To clamber on top of one of the cubes, so as to be able to jump the Arena wall, go to 57.

77 | Martha leads you quickly along the corridor. As you enter a new sector, you pass a series of what look like fitness suites, full of futuristic exercise equipment. You guess this is where the Group Nine prison officers formerly kept in shape.

The passageway begins to climb gently, and you struggle to keep pace with Martha, who is striding out determinedly.

A little further along, a slim silver plinth stands in the centre of the corridor. Mounted on top of it is a perfect, jet-black sphere.

'What's that, d'ya reckon?' you ask as you approach the statue-like object.

Martha peers curiously at the sphere, and shrugs. 'Beats me. Some sort of artwork, perhaps? Anyway, let's crack on.'

Without further ado, she carries on along the passageway.

To continue along the corridor with Martha, go to 85. To take a closer look at the unusual statue, go to 2.

You cling desperately to your opponent's powerful forelimb. Suddenly, its other monstrous pincer comes scything towards you. With split-second timing, you yank the limb you are holding sharply forward, then release your grip.

As you hit the floor hard, a tormented alien howl fills the Arena. Thanks to your clever manoeuvre, the creature's attempt to slice you in half has failed. Instead, it has cut off one of its own giant pincers. The severed claw lies on the floor beside you.

But even as you watch, a replacement claw begins to slowly regrow, impossibly, at the end of your opponent's damaged limb.

Horrified, you scramble to your feet as the creature renews its attack, now more furious than ever.

To use the severed claw to fend off blows from the intact one, go to 89. To try once again to get away from the wounded creature, go to 83.

As the Doctor strides out purposefully, you accompany him, and quickly find yourself in an area of the ship quite unlike the last — white-walled, spotless, with a clearly clinical feel.

'Medical Bay,' confirms the Doctor. He crosses to peer through a pair of double doors in one wall. 'Operating theatre. Very impressive. On a long haul through deep-space, you need the full shebang, I guess. They've even got a Cryogenic Vault.'

He gestures to a pair of transparent sliding doors in the opposite wall.

'If anyone's too sick or injured to be cured on-board, they whack them in the deep freeze until they can dock somewhere with better facilities.'

He begins rummaging through a cabinet of bottles and packets.

'Wonder if they've got anything for a bad headache…'

To take a look at the Cryogenic area, go to 70. To enter the Operating Theatre, go to 49.

You quickly scale the gantry ladder, hauling yourself up rung after rung until you reach the walkway that runs across beneath the hanger roof. The two aliens pursuing you have now entered the hangar, and are hurriedly climbing the ladder behind you.

To your horror, you see that their loud grunting has raised the alarm. A pair of reptilian creatures, with slit-eyes and lolling red tongues, come slinking onto the gantry walkway from the exit at its other end. They spot you immediately, and begin to approach menacingly, on all fours. Behind you, your two original followers have reached the top of the ladder. You are trapped.

There is one, rather desperate, possibility for escape. The gantry is six or seven metres above the hangar floor. There is a slim chance you could survive the drop.

To make the jump, go to 16. To stand and fight, go to 33.

You make it across the canteen without being spotted, and slip through a doorway in the far wall. It leads into what you quickly realise is a kitchen area, packed with hi-tech food preparation devices. It's in a disgusting state, littered with unfinished meals, jugs of orange dregs, and part-emptied drums of frying oil.

There is an exit at one end of the kitchen. At the other end, an enormous, bear-like creature is greedily rooting through a pile of scraps. It suddenly spots you. After a momentary pause, it gives a blood-curdling roar, and gleaming, foot-long claws emerge from its massive paws.

You spot the opening of a ventilation shaft in the wall beside you – too narrow for the massive creature to fit through.

To spill frying oil over the floor to delay your assailant, then dash for the exit, go to 88. To escape via the ventilation shaft, go to 21.

82 You find yourself in a large, circular room. The far wall is transparent, forming a vast viewing window. Through it you can see a black void beyond, speckled with pinpricks of light. You are clearly looking out into deep space.

At the centre of the room stands a raised circular plinth. Its upper surface is inky black, crisscrossed by bright green gridlines. A tiny yellow and silver spacecraft — a 3-D projection — hovers impossibly above the luminous grid's central axes. Holographs of miniature planets, circled by tiny moons, float elsewhere, creating a sophisticated astronomical map.

Around the walls are banks of electronic equipment. Displays blink with technical read-outs and animated diagrams. This is clearly some sort of control centre, but it appears to be deserted.

You cross to a lift that stands open in one wall. It has two control buttons.

To press the button marked CLASSIFIED, go to 28. To press ENGINEERING, go to 58.

You evade your monstrous opponent once again. But it is quick to resume the attack, and you are running out of hope.

Suddenly, what looks like a Christmas tree bauble lands at your opponent's feet, much to its bewilderment. An instant later, the bauble explodes, temporarily stunning your enemy. A second explosion goes off nearby, and you turn to see Martha's opponent also reeling in dazed confusion.

'Quick! Over here!'

The Doctor is standing beside Jal-Neth in the mouth of the Arena's exit tunnel. As you and Martha race to join them, several of the angry crowd open fire. Plasma blasts erupt around you, but you make it to the exit unhurt.

The Doctor hurriedly leads you through a sequence of corridors before bursting into a familiar room — the room where you first arrived. The Extraction Device stands at its centre, its fluid-filled tubes bubbling gently.

As Jal-Neth and Martha jam the door, the Doctor immediately begins operating the Extraction Device's control console.

'The solution's simple, really. Mr Big has caused severe temporal disruption with this device of his. To remedy the situation, all we have to do is to use the device to extract him from time, prior to its invention — so it never gets made. It will create a short-term time paradox, of course — probably cause Big some memory malfunction. But more importantly, it will release anyone who he has extracted — like you — back to their own times. It will be like none of this ever happened.'

The Doctor looks up from the console.

'So — ready to erase all this?'

You nod. The Doctor flashes you a broad grin, then touches a control screen. The room vanishes in an explosion of light.

You are striding along the rain-soaked pavement, heading for school — the beginning of another typical day.

Just for once, you wish something unusual would happen…

The End

84 You draw on all your speed and agility to keep one step ahead of your monstrous opponent, but the empty Arena offers nowhere to hide, and you are beginning to tire.

As you duck, dodge and dive to avoid slashing claws and deadly tail strikes, you are driven back against one of the Arena walls.

'Stand and fight!' taunts Mr Big, yelling from among the jeering crowd behind you. 'We didn't come to see a dance!'

'Then give me something to fight with!' you scream back angrily.

In response, a slim, ultra-modern fighting-staff is flung from somewhere in the crowd to land on the Arena floor a few metres from where you stand.

To grab the staff and attempt to fend off your opponent, go to 72. To continue dodging, hoping the creature will eventually tire, go to 83.

The corridor abruptly branches into two.

'Where now?'

Martha ponders for a moment.

'Dunno. We'll have to split up.' She gestures to the left. 'You try that way. If you run into trouble, yell like crazy. I'll meet you back here in ten minutes — OK?'

Flashing you an encouraging smile, she sets off along the right fork.

Fifty metres further on, you encounter a figure slumped against the passage wall. It's a convict, but human — a large, burly man. He has a foul-smelling flask grasped in one hand, and is snoring loudly.

Clipped to the drunk's belt is a yellow and silver gadget with a screen and keypad, bearing a Group Nine logo — a portable surveillance device. If you could remove it without waking the man, it might help you locate the TARDIS, Jal-Neth, or your enemies' whereabouts.

To continue along the corridor, go to 51.
To risk pinching the surveillance gadget, go to 56.

The corridor leads to a pyramid-shaped room. Peering in cautiously, you notice the unusual floor — it reminds you of an old-fashioned camera shutter, with several overlapping curved segments. There is a circular opening in the centre of each of the room's triangular walls.

The apex of the pyramid suddenly opens, and a stream of rubbish tumbles through. Robotic arms instantly emerge from the walls and begin to sift through the refuse, plucking out items and depositing them into one of the openings in the walls. It's an automated waste-sorting process — each hole is a chute for a specific kind of recyclable material.

Their job done, the arms withdraw, and the entire floor momentarily spirals open, to let the remaining rubbish drop through.

You are suddenly aware of footsteps in the corridor behind you. Someone is approaching.

To dive down the nearest chute, go to 68. To confront whoever is approaching, go to 5.

The passageway leads to a pair of badly damaged security doors, labelled 'Sector K45'. Beyond them, the corridor widens, and is lined with black cell doors at regular intervals on both sides.

Mounted on the wall is a large touchscreen, showing a schematic diagram.

'Looks like a cell layout,' whispers the Doctor. His fingers expertly navigate the touchscreen. 'Let's see what undesirables they've got locked up...'

Details of the first cell's occupant flash up on the screen — an image of an ancient Japanese samurai:

Name: Ryu Arashi. Extraction data: Earth, Year 537.

The next data record shows a monstrous slug-like creature with triple rows of teeth in its vast, drooling mouth:

Name: Praklav III. Extraction data: Troth, Year 200890.

'But how did they get here...?' murmurs the Doctor. 'Or rather, now...?'

To continue along the corridor, go to 97. To look further through the prisoner database, go to 62.

Your plan works, enabling you to make your escape. You soon find yourself on the threshold of a hexagonal room with doorways in two of its other walls.

Perched awkwardly at a control console in the centre of the room, with his back to you, sits Mr Big. He is watching the far wall, on which is projected the unlikely image of an old-fashioned police phone box. Sitting beside Big is another inhuman figure. It reminds you of a large newt, with moist skin and gill-like frills at its neck.

'So what is it, Plux?' Mr Big asks brusquely. 'It looks wooden. That makes it at least 25,000 years old. What's it doing in 30506, on my ship?'

'It's a spacecraft, of sorts,' replies the newt creature. 'I've been through our ship's data archive, and found several matches. It's called the TARDIS. Belongs to a very interesting individual. The Doctor. Surviving member of a race known as the Time Lords. Able to regenerate into renewed physical form. His current manifestation is …'

'Well, whoever he is, I want him caught — quickly,' snaps Mr Big. 'You have his companion already, yes?'

'Yes, boss.' An attractive young woman appears on the wall. 'Calls herself Martha, but we've been unable to get anything else out of her so far. She's being held in Sector K45.'

You're startled to hear a third voice just behind you.

'K45. Thanks for that!'

You turn to see the pinstripe-suited man standing just behind you. He gives Mr Big a cheeky mock salute, then dashes for the nearest exit.

'After them!' yells Mr Big, furious.

To follow the Doctor, go to 24. To make a break for the other exit, go to 86.

Your desperate measures buy you a little more time. But before long, you are once more at the mercy of your alien opponent.

Suddenly, a high-pitched whirring sound grabs your attention. You look up to see the Doctor plummeting from the domed ceiling high above. He is suspended from a service gantry by a thin cable, which is rapidly unreeling from a spooling device at his waist.

'Thought I'd just drop in,' grins the Doctor, landing. 'Grab hold!'

You quickly clasp your arms around the Doctor's neck. As he activates the line-spooler, the two of you shoot upwards. Nearby, you notice Jal-Neth hoisting Martha to safety in a similar dramatic fashion.

As the four of you reach the safety of the ceiling gantry, the Doctor pulls his sonic screwdriver from his pocket and presses one of its buttons. A shimmering dome of energy suddenly blossoms below you, encapsulating the entire Arena — including the area where the crowd are gathered.

You watch as several of the convicts charge at the energy barrier, only to recoil, badly stunned.

'Area Containment Field,' explains the Doctor. 'It's a security feature of the ship. Big's 'Arena' was originally the prisoner exercise area. Group Nine are smart enough to know that when you put prisoners together, it's a recipe for trouble. Renders all electromagnetic weapons within it inoperable, too.'

He points the screwdriver again.

'Watch this.'

As one, the transparent cubes around the Arena's perimeter dissolve away, freeing their occupants. You are soon enjoying the sight of Mr Big, stungun discarded, desperately trying to evade an angry, club-wielding warrior within the confines of the Containment Field below.

'I've set it to cut out in twenty-four hours. That should be long enough for our abducted friends to persuade Mr Big to return them to their original times, don't you think?'

The Doctor puts his arm around your shoulder. 'In the meantime, how do you fancy a trip home in the TARDIS? Can't promise we'll hit the twenty-first century first time, but it should be an interesting ride ...'

This adventure is over, but where will the TARDIS take you next time?

The ladder takes you and the Doctor down into a dimly lit storage area. It is crammed with technical supplies, from fluid-filled canisters to crates of fuel-cells. Stacks of thick hexagonal tiles, with an opaque black surface, stand everywhere.

'Dissipation Cells,' mutters the Doctor distractedly, scanning the room for another exit. 'They can soak up extreme heat, or other kinds of excess energy. Used to protect a starship's hull. These are spares, I guess.'

There's a clank-clank, as a pair of clawed feet begin to descend the ladder rungs above you. The aliens who shot Martha are clearly on your tail.

'There!' yells the Doctor, pointing wildly to a doorway in the far wall. 'Run! I'll hold them up for a while!'

To head for the exit corridor, go to 19.
To stand your ground with the Doctor, go to 48.

As you burst through the fake wall, you are beset by thousands of tiny luminous orange particles. Travelling at lightning speed, they ricochet off the walls, floor and ceilings of the corridor. Each one that strikes you creates a painful, stinging sensation.

'So there was something nasty behind it,' observes the Doctor, wincing from the bombardment. 'Someone must have detonated a Sunburst Grenade here recently. They've tried to contain the aftermath with energy barriers — these fake walls.'

He gestures to another wall across the corridor twenty metres ahead. Midway between the walls, a fragmented canister lies on the floor.

'It'll get much worse nearer the grenade — probably lethal. We'll have to go back.'

You move hastily back through the wall — only to come face to face with several large, angry-looking alien convicts.

To stand and fight, go to 26. To try to dodge past them, go to 44.

As you peer beneath the tables ahead, through a forest of peculiar, inhuman legs, you can make out the lower part of an exit passageway, on the opposite side of the hall.

Above you, one of the aliens belches loudly.

'How d'ya reckon Big's getting 'old of all these ancient types, then?'

'Dunno. Some sort of time transfer gadget, I guess. You know that smart-alec Darillian fella — skinny orange, all legs and eyes, got banged up for shipping dodgy biotech parts?'

'Uh-huh.'

'Well, Big 'ad 'im tinkering away in the old medical labs. Bet it's 'im what's done it.'

You unintentionally knock the underside of the table with the back of your head.

'Whassat?' grunts the larger alien.

To crawl rapidly under the tables to the exit passage, go to 21. To break from cover, and run for it, go to 33.

93 However hard you try, it seems impossible to put any distance between yourself and your alien opponent's lethal claws. Regardless of how you twist, turn, duck and dive, the giant, serrated-edged pincers snap relentlessly at you, missing by millimetres.

As the creature lunges at you yet again with a terrible claw, you decide to try a daring tactic. You sidestep the claw, then grab hold of the monster's limb just behind it. As the creature withdraws its pincer to strike again, you cling on desperately.

Surprised, and very annoyed, the monster shakes its powerful limb wildly back and forth to dislodge you, throwing you left and right, up and down, like a rag doll.

To cling on for dear life, go to 78. To let go, go to 6.

The diversion works beautifully — the aliens guarding the cell door hurry away to deal with the crisis. With the coast clear, you and the Doctor rush to Martha's cell to attempt to set her free.

The Doctor pulls a slim silver device, a bit like a torch, from one of his jacket pockets.

'Sonic screwdriver,' he explains, seeing your inquisitive look. 'Sort of electronic Swiss army knife.'

He touches the luminous blue end of the gadget on the lock keypad. An instant later, the door hisses open.

'Doctor!'

Martha bursts out of the cell, clearly delighted to see her friend. Then a second figure steps out behind her. It is a young man, dressed in a yellow and silver uniform.

'Much obliged, Doctor,' he says. 'Now, if you'll excuse me, I have a score to settle with Mr Big.' And with that, he jogs away along the corridor.

'He's a Group Nine prison officer,' explains Martha, 'Called Jal-Neth. He was one of the crew of this prison transport ship when the convict inmates staged a mass revolt and took it over. Their leader is someone called Mr Big. Since he seized control, he's apparently developed some kind of machine that can extract people from time. He's using it to collect famous warriors, from all kinds of places. Jal-Neth says the cells are packed with them. Then he stages contests between them, making a killing on the gambling.'

The Doctor looks worried. 'If Big really is running an Extraction Device — which would explain our young friend here — then we need to put it out of action, and quickly. You can't just pull people willy-nilly out of history. The damage to the space-time continuum could be catastrophic...'

'You deal with the machine — I'm going after Jal-Neth,' says Martha, determinedly. 'He's going to need all the help he can get.'

To go with Martha, go to 42. To help the Doctor, go to 79.

The corridor ends at a pair of sturdy sliding doors. As you approach them, an electronic voice addresses you.

'This is a classified area. Retinal identification is required. Please look directly into the ID screen.'

A sliding panel reveals a small screen in the wall beside the doors. As you stare at the screen, it projects a thin red beam directly into your right eye.

For a few seconds, images of men and women in yellow and silver uniforms, with their names and serial numbers, flicker momentarily across the screen. Then it falls blank once more.

'Personnel match unsuccessful. Your presence on board the Group Nine Starship Custodian is unauthorised. Please remain where you are.'

A second set of blast-proof doors suddenly slam shut across the first, and a deafening alarm wails into life.

To run for it, go to 31. To hide in the shadowed alcove in one wall of the corridor, go to 36.

You and Martha turn and run headlong at your heavily-armoured opponent, screaming wildly. The creature looks somewhat taken aback, then raises its spear and launches it fiercely at Martha.

'Look out!'

Martha sidesteps, and the spear shoots harmlessly past. An instant later, it buries itself in the thigh of her human opponent, who had been pursuing her.

The warrior drops his sword and shield, clasps the shaft of the spear, and pulls it from his leg with a roar of pain. Eyes full of rage, he breaks the spear over his other knee, and flings its fragments back towards you.

'Now he's really mad,' murmurs Martha. She hastily snatches up one half of the broken spear as a makeshift weapon, as her wounded opponent engages her in battle once more.

To grab the other part of the spear, to fend off your opponent, go to 72. To beat a hasty retreat, go to 83.

A short way ahead, another passageway branches off to the left. From around the corner, you can hear two gruff voices in conversation.

'What's Big want with some weedy human female, anyway?'

'Dunno. Just told us to guard her "till otherwise instructed".'

The Doctor grasps your arm. 'I think we've found Martha,' he whispers. Then, to your horror, he strides boldly around the corner, bundling you forward with him. As the two surprised convicts guarding Martha's cell spin round, the Doctor addresses them jovially.

'OK boys — we'll take it from here.' Despite the guards' bemused scowls, the Doctor continues cheerily. 'They need you up in Sector L7 — couple of extractees gone loco — Mr Big's orders.'

The convicts, neither of whom seem too bright, look at one another uncertainly, then back at the Doctor's beaming face.

> **To stand your ground, sticking with the Doctor's bluff, go to 94. To run for it, go to 44.**

You reach a section of the corridor where angry noises are coming from inside many of the cells. Peering through one door window, you see a vast black-furred hulk in full body armour, pounding its bed to smithereens. Another cell holds a Japanese samurai, rehearsing complex combat moves and blood-curdling battle cries.

The sound of approaching footsteps puts you on instant alert. Two alien ruffians are escorting a third figure — a human — along the corridor. Their prisoner reminds you uncannily of a picture you once saw of twelfth century Mongol warlord Genghis Khan.

As his captors' attention briefly falls on you, the prisoner seizes his chance. Snatching his heavy club from one alien, he floors them both with lightning-fast blows. Then he charges along the corridor towards you, club whirling.

To stand your ground, go to 16. To attempt the classic 'Look out — behind you!' diversion, then run like the wind, go to 88.

You snatch up the battered shield — made of thick, metal-studded timber — while your opponent angrily attempts to regain its vision.

Giving a blood-curdling howl of rage, the creature finally tears your jacket away from its face. With its single unblinking eye able to see again, it rounds on you angrily, then unleashes another ferocious attack with its laser-tipped weapon.

You somehow manage to block the flurry of violent blows raining down on you with the shield. But its primitive construction is no match for your enemy's hi-tech weapon. Its vicious jabs and slashes splinter and scorch the wood. The shield won't stand many more hits before it no longer offers you any protection.

To use the shield to fend off the next attack, go to 72. To throw it as hard as you can at your opponent's alien face, then run for it, go to 83.

Don't miss these other exciting adventures with the Doctor!

Coming soon...